DATE DUE

OCT 14 1986	DEC 2 0		
NOV 6 1986	MAR 9 1990		
NOV 13 1986	AR. 30		
NOV 2 6 1986	JAN 1 1 1991		
DEC 2 1986	APR. 8 1991		
JAN 2 4 1987	DEC 4 '91		
FEB 1 1989	DEC 1 8 91		
MAR 3 1989	JAN 26 93		
MAY 15 1989	SEP 3 0 1998		
OCT 5 1989	FEB 1 0 1999		
NOV 8 1989			
NOV 2 2 1989	NOV - 1 2000		
	NOV 1 5 2001		

C-2

Fic   Billington, Elizabeth T.
BIL   Part-time boy

PART-TIME BOY

Elizabeth T. Billington

PART-TIME BOY

ILLUSTRATED BY
Diane de Groat

FREDERICK WARNE
New York   London

Frederick Warne & Co., Inc.
New York, New York
Library of Congress Cataloging in Publication Data
Billington, Elizabeth T.
Part-time boy.
Summary: Jamie, a quiet individualist in a noisy family,
finds friendship, understanding, and a new self-confidence
during the summer he spends in the country
with an unusual young woman.
[1. Friendship—Fictional] I. DeGroat, Diane.
II. Title.
PZ7.B4993Par   [Fic]   79–23273
ISBN 0–7232–6175–X
Printed in the U.S.A. by Maple Press
Book design by Kathleen Westray
1   2   3   4   5   84   83   82   81   80

FOR JIM

who kindly lets me care for his cat

CHAPTER

I

I watched the salesman's face as I walked into the shoe store followed by my brothers Carl and Paul. Mom came in last, but before she did, Carl reached up and kept his finger on the signal buzzer, which makes the bell ring without stopping. The salesman didn't need a signal to know we'd come in because Paul tripped over his own feet and sent a pile of empty shoeboxes all over the floor. It seemed to me the salesman's face fell apart and then tightened up again. The feeling I got was that he was sorry we'd come.

"They all need summer shoes," Mom announced as we sat down in a row.

"Let's take care of the little guy first," the man said, pushing a low stool in front of me. *The little guy.* That's me. I'd thought a long time about getting new shoes, and so I knew just what I wanted and spoke right up.

"I want desert boots," I said in a loud voice as I slid down in the chair, hunching my shoulders around my ears.

"He spoke! The little guy spoke!" Paul raised his arms high in the air. Paul's always acting.

"Gee," Carl said, "what d'ya want desert boots for, Jamie? You're not going to the desert. People don't wear desert boots in the summer."

"Cut it out," Mom ordered. "Jamie may have desert boots if that's what he wants."

Carl and Paul squirmed like they were in great pain or dying.

"Desert boots." Carl shook his head. "No wonder the kids in school call you 'Dumb-Dumb.' Dumb 'cause you won't talk and dumb 'cause you always have to be different."

Mom took a long, slow breath as she tapped her fingers on the arm of the chair. She was trying to keep calm.

The salesman brought the desert boots and helped me put them on. He checked the fit and made me walk along the store in the boots. They were made of a rough leather and came over my ankles. They felt stiff and heavy, but the man said they fit good.

"Keep them on, wear them home," Mom ordered. She opened her wallet and gave me two dollars. "Go buy yourself something; we'll meet you outside." Mom wanted me out of the way.

I walked along the sidewalk, getting used to the feel of the boots as I looked in store windows. I was all the way to the corner store before I saw what I wanted to buy.

High up in the back of the store window was a bright orange hat. It was different from any hat I'd ever seen. It came to a peak and had a long, colored feather on one side. I looked at it carefully, then I went into the store. I had enough money to buy the hat, so I did. I put the hat on and went outside, all the while looking at myself in the glass of the store window. What a hat. Better than my cowboy hat, I thought. I felt pleased.

In every store window I passed, I looked at myself, admiring my hat. I got to the shoe store just as Carl came out. He was wearing bright red sneakers and kind of jogging in place to try them out. He stopped jogging.

"What a freak! An elf's hat and desert boots." Carl sounded disgusted.

Carl hates it when I look different. He knows,

as I do, that people notice right away if you're different. He doesn't like that. It doesn't bother me.

I said nothing. We stood looking at each other till Paul and Mom came out of the store. Paul acted out a big double take.

"I don't believe my eyes," he said. "What is *that*?"

Before Carl could answer him, Mom interrupted. "Let him alone. It's better than the football helmet he's worn all winter."

And she was right.

When Dad got home from work that evening, I was sitting on the steps, wearing my new hat.

"Hey, Jamie, where'd you get that hat?" Dad asked as he climbed out of the car.

Without waiting for me to answer, he started talking as he came over to sit next to me. I took off the hat so he could look at it. While he held it, he told me it was a Tyrolean hat, the kind worn by people who climb the high mountains of Austria.

Silently I repeated over and over in my head the words "Tyrolean hat." I didn't want to forget that name. My dad's a great guy. He always tells me something special about things I have.

PART-TIME BOY

Mom never lets me wear a hat at the dinner table, so before we sat down I put the Tyrolean hat over one of the pewter candlesticks on the buffet. That way I could look at the hat while I ate dinner. Dinner at our house is noisy and mixed-up. Carl and Paul talk and kid around, and so it gets very loud sometimes.

"Let's keep the noise level down," Dad says now and then.

"Don't eat so fast," seems to be all Mom can say.

Me, I just sit and eat. That night I kept saying "Tyrolean hat" over and over in my mind as I looked at it. I thought the orange was a lovely color against the blue and white wallpaper. I kind of jumped when I realized Mom was talking to me.

"Jamie, are you all right?" she asked.

I looked at her and smiled as I nodded. I know Mom worries because I don't talk. She doesn't understand that I don't have a lot to say.

When dinner was over, I picked up my hat and rubbed my hand over the orange material. I smoothed the feather with my fingers. It was a great hat. I put it on and went to sit on the steps to watch Carl and Paul throw the frisbee in the garden.

PART-TIME BOY

When I got in bed, the words "Tyrolean hat" still kept going through my mind. I liked those words. Out of nowhere an idea came. I'd be a mountain climber. Right in back of our house is a steep hill. Tomorrow was Saturday, so there was no school. I'd climb the road to the top of the hill and pretend I was a Tyrolean mountain climber.

In the light that came through my window from the street lamp, I could see the hat with its long feather where I'd put it on top of my dresser before I got into bed. I just knew I was going to have a good time with that hat.

CHAPTER
2

My Tyrolean hat was the first thing I saw when I opened my eyes Saturday morning. It was sunny and hot, even though it was still early. I had a good feeling inside me as I lifted the hat down from the dresser and put it on. I went downstairs in my pajamas to see what we were having for breakfast.

Mom was in the kitchen alone, loading the dishwasher. Carl and Paul had eaten earlier with Dad, and they had all gone to play ball at the schoolyard.

"Morning, Jamie. Did you sleep in your new hat?" Mom asked.

I shook my head. I knew Mom was teasing. She even let me wear my hat while I ate breakfast at the kitchen table.

It was the middle of the morning before I

walked down the street wearing my Tyrolean hat. I turned the corner and started the long climb up the hill all by myself, which is the way I do things. I'd never been up this hill before. It was steeper and longer than I thought.

When I got to the top, I was panting, sweating, and scared. I felt like I was going to throw up. I sat on a ledge of rock by the side of the cement walk to cool off and think. I swallowed hard and pushed the hat back on my sweaty head. I wanted to figure out why I was scared. I scared myself sometimes when I pretended to drive a stagecoach and the horses would run faster and faster down a steep narrow road. Climbing the hill, I had pretended nothing. I'd been too busy climbing.

One thing I knew for sure: I wasn't afraid of being alone. Maybe, I thought, I feel lost. I knew I wasn't lost—our house was down the hill and around the corner. I closed my eyes so I could picture our house.

I was sitting there with my eyes closed when I heard a sound. Not a loud noise; just a kind of rustling in the grass in back of me. Not turning around, I wondered if it could be a tiger, escaped from a circus, getting ready to jump me. I was pretending again. I'd better stop.

I turned to see a black and white cat pushing through the grass at the side of the ledge. Slowly, silently, the cat sat down. It put its white front feet together and curled its black tail around them. From behind a mask of black fur, the cat stared at me. I stared back.

After a while the cat stood up, stretched, and came toward me. It stopped to rub the side of its head on the far side of the ledge. Tired of that, the cat rolled over on its back and wriggled around. I guessed it wanted me to stroke its stomach. I went over and stooped down. Gently I stroked the soft white fur on its stomach. The cat started to purr loudly. I felt real happy. The scared feeling was gone.

The cat got up and walked to the grass at the back of the ledge. Its tail was straight up in the air with just the tip turned over to one side. *Follow me,* it seemed to signal.

I followed and saw a narrow path that I hadn't seen from the road. I walked along the grass path following the cat; its black back had two fine lines of white fur running across the middle. The lines moved as the cat walked. There was no way I could guess that those lines would help it make a friend as well as save its life in the coming summer.

Tall brambles started to cover the path. They caught my shirt and even my hat with their thorns. Suddenly I couldn't see the cat. Instead of brambles, there was a high, thick hedge in front of me.

I stooped and saw an opening in the bottom of the hedge. The cat must've squeezed through. I took off my hat so I could lie down flat and look through the opening. In the sunny open space on the far side of the hedge I saw the cat rubbing against the blue jeans of a woman who was digging in the ground.

"Hi, Sukie," the woman said. "Where have you been?"

Tail up, Sukie started back toward the hedge.

"O.K., I'll come and see what you've brought this time," said the woman.

She stuck the fork she'd used for digging into the newly turned earth and came toward the hedge. I tried to squirm back out of the way, but I was stuck. The woman bent forward and looked through the opening. I looked into the bluest eyes I'd ever seen.

"Why, it's a boy!" she exclaimed. "Come on through. Let me see you."

I pulled myself along with my elbows, dragging my hat behind me. I got through the hedge and stood up. The feather on my hat was pulled all apart. I guessed it was ruined.

"Here," said the woman, taking my hat, "I'll fix the feather for you. There are little hooks all along the edge of the feather and they hold it together."

She ran her hand along the feather. It looked as good as new. I took the hat from her and put it on. The woman pushed back her long blond hair with both hands.

"I'm Mattie Swenson," she said. "Who are you?"

I looked at her for a minute. "Jamie Johnson," I answered.

Mattie crossed her legs and sat down smooth as could be. I crossed my legs and sat down next to her, not so smooth. Sukie rubbed against my knee, purring. I stroked the cat.

"Where do you live, Jamie?" Mattie asked.

"Down the hill and around the corner," I told her.

"The big white house where there are always a lot of boys playing?"

I nodded.

"Can you stay for a while? Will anyone be missing you?" she asked.

I pushed my hat back on my head and sat there, thinking. I didn't think anyone would miss me. I was too old to be just a little kid, but too young to be an adolescent like Carl and Paul. I was me, all by myself. Mom and Dad don't worry where I go; I'm ten.

"I can stay," I said softly.

"That's good," said Mattie, getting up from the ground.

I got up too, and we both followed Sukie, who ran along, tail in the air. It was like a game—Sukie was leader, and we had to follow. Sukie led us to a large wire cage that was held up in the air by big wooden posts. The cage had no floor, just wire. Inside were two large reddish rabbits. I never knew there were rabbits that color.

"Meet Cinnamon and Ginger," said Mattie. "They're visiting me because their owner is away. Part-time rabbits, I call them."

Mattie opened a wire door and reached in,

picking up one of the rabbits. Then she closed the door and sat on the ground, holding the rabbit in her arms and stroking its head. I watched for a few minutes before I put out my hand and stroked the rabbit's back. The rabbit's nose kept twitching; I thought it was going to sneeze.

"Cinnamon likes you," Mattie said. "I wonder if that's because you have red hair and brown eyes like he does."

I liked that idea and grinned at Mattie as I shrugged my shoulders. Then Mattie put the rabbit back in the cage, and we went over to a small shed at the edge of the yard where Sukie was sniffing at a turtle in the shed doorway.

"You might call that my part-time turtle," said Mattie. "The turtle lives in the lake all summer, eating and raising a family, but it visits me here in the spring."

Sukie was rubbing on a wire fence that closed off the back of the yard. Mattie leaned on the frame of the gate in the middle of the fence.

"I had to fence this part when I brought home some part-time goats," she said. "As it turned out, I soon had a part-time lamb and a couple of geese. They are from the Natural Science Center—that's where I work. I bring them here to give them a rest from their human visitors."

We followed Sukie toward the house. I had a nice feeling all over me. I was having an adventure.

"Want a drink?" asked Mattie.

I nodded. The climb had made me thirsty as well as hot. "Please," I remembered to say.

Mattie shooed Sukie away from the door where she had been waiting.

"You stay out here, Sukie," she said.

We went into a big room. There was stuff all over the place. Mom would have called it a mess. I took off my hat and put it on an empty chair. I looked around. Mattie pushed books, tools, clothes, and jars across the table with her arm so that we would have room to eat. She gave me a box of cookies and a couple of paper napkins. I put some cookies on the napkins while she washed two glasses from the pile of dirty dishes in the sink. That done, Mattie poured milk for us to drink and we sat at the table.

I hadn't taken one bite out of the cookies when I suddenly stopped breathing. There was a fluttering sound and a flash of color near my head. A bird was sitting on my shoulder, pulling the hair on my neck. I wasn't sure I liked that.

"That's Charlotte. She won't hurt you," Mattie said. "I see Charlotte likes red hair too."

I kind of twisted my head around and saw a bright green bird.

"Charlotte is a part-time parakeet. Her people are away. I don't take care of many birds now that Sukie lives with me. Sukie was a part-time cat, but when the time came for her to go home, she refused to leave. Sukie has lived here ever since," Mattie explained.

I sat listening to the noises the parakeet was making. They sounded like words. The bird was talking!

"Pretty bird, pretty bird, pretty bird," the parakeet was saying over and over.

"Charlotte is talking to me," I gasped.

Mattie laughed out loud. "I know," Mattie said. "Crumble some cookie on the table for her."

I crushed a piece of cookie with my finger, and Charlotte flew down to eat the crumbs. Without a word, Mattie and I watched.

I thought about going home but didn't know what to say. I stood up, took my hat, and started toward the door. "I gotta go," I said.

"O.K.," Mattie said, closing her hand right over Charlotte and then climbing on a chair to put Charlotte in a cage high over our heads. Mattie jumped off the chair and came with me to the door.

"You can go down the driveway to the road," Mattie said. "There's no need to crawl back under the hedge."

I put on my hat and nodded. I walked down the drive.

"Come back soon," Mattie called.

Sukie appeared out of the bushes at the end of the drive. She walked ahead of me to the rock ledge where we had met. She jumped onto the rock and sat there neatly. I rubbed her head while she purred.

I walked down the hill backward, watching Sukie all the time. At the bottom, by squinting my eyes, I could see her black and white figure on the rock. I thought she was watching me.

I turned the corner. Mountain climbing had found me two friends. Who could tell what would happen next?

PART-TIME BOY

CHAPTER

3

Sunday afternoon was quiet at our house. I stood on the porch wondering what I'd do when, in my head, I heard Mattie's voice saying, "Come back soon." I knew she'd meant it, and so I walked up the hill to her house.

Sukie came running and gave a *prrr-rr-oo* of happiness when she saw me. Mattie, who was still digging in her garden, smiled, and her blue eyes shone and sparkled as I approached.

In the weeks that followed, I went to Mattie's house a lot of times. Time got mixed-up for me. Instead of going to school, coming home, and watching Carl and Paul or pretending, I became Mattie's helper. She always needed me for something.

When the garden was dug over, I helped plant carrots, lettuce, radishes, corn, beans, pumpkins, and other things. The day I saw the little green shoots come through the soil I was thrilled. I'd never seen that before.

On rainy days we worked inside. Mattie was building a closet in what used to be the front entrance to her house. I was her carpenter's helper.

"With just two rooms I don't need two doors to come in and out," she explained, "but I sure as heck need a closet."

At home, Paul and Carl were getting ready for summer. They were going to Jamboree. Even though they talked Jamboree all the time, I didn't understand what Jamboree was or why it was special. I just knew it was. Mom was making a flag for them to put on their tent. Dad was always looking at catalogs and talking about "buying gear" or "checking gear." I had no part of Jamboree. All I did was watch and listen.

One real hot night I couldn't sleep. Paul and Carl were talking softly in the room next to mine. I knew they were talking Jamboree. I felt a little lonely and left out. I could hear Mom and Dad talking as they sat on the side porch below my window. I thought I'd be cooler sitting on the bottom step of the stairs in the dark hall, so I got out of bed and crept silently down the stairs. For a few minutes I listened to Mom and Dad talking. They were talking about me!

"You just don't seem to understand. I'm worried about Jamie," Mom said. "He seldom says a word. The boys don't ask him to play—in fact, they act as if he wasn't there. I think Jamie feels left out and unhappy."

"I try to understand, Marian," Dad replied. "But, you see, Jamie seems happy enough to me. He likes to be alone, to listen and watch. I notice he speaks when he has something to say, but not otherwise."

"There's nothing wrong with his being alone sometimes," Mom replied. "It's just that I feel he's lonely at times. Given the chance, Paul and Carl tease him unmercifully. Jamie doesn't try to get back at them or even come running to me. He just goes off on his own without a word. He seems to live in another world. And he's young for his age. I—"

Dad interrupted her. "I know why you're upset, Marian. It's his school report, isn't it? Let me tell you something. That report doesn't say a thing we don't already know. It says, 'Jamie is not working to his capacity.' Well, show me a kid who does. And the last remark, 'Jamie is a loner, he does not participate in the group and resists any encouragement to do so.' So what's wrong with being a loner? I tell you, Marian, the other two boys and their million friends are always underfoot and never shut up! Jamie is a welcome relief. Jamie *is* young, and I'll take Jamie's kind any day."

Dad sounded cross. He was real serious, I know, because he doesn't call Mom "Marian" unless he means business.

"Jamie will be all alone when school is out," Mom said. "Carl and Paul will be away, and the two boys down the road are going to camp all summer."

Dad gave a big sigh. "Jamie doesn't play with those boys anyway. Let Jamie alone, Marian."

Mom didn't answer.

"I'll tell you something you and his teacher haven't noticed," Dad said after a few minutes. "Jamie has changed in the past weeks. He's not sitting on the step watching the other boys while he waits for me to come home from work. Instead, he's off somewhere. I've seen him disappear up Hill Road on weekends. I don't know what or who is up there, but Jamie'll tell us when he's ready. Have you noticed how he's started to do things without being asked? This evening it was Jamie who ran down the steps to carry the grocery bag into the kitchen when you came home. Jamie is growing up just fine."

Without a sound I backed up the stairs, got into bed, and sat hugging my knees. I rocked back and forth. A lot of different ideas were going around and around in my head. I felt like crying because Mom didn't like me the way I am. I felt sad about not fitting in at home or at school. I thought, Mattie likes me the way I am. Mattie was going to her part-time home this summer. I wondered if I could go with her and be her part-time boy. I fell asleep thinking of how I'd ask Mattie about it tomorrow.

The next day at school was terrible. I was tired because I'd been awake so late. It was hot, and I thought the afternoon would go on forever. When I got home, Mom had a couple of friends with her in the living room where the Jamboree flag was spread on the rug. They were so busy ooh-ing and aah-ing that it was easy for me to go to Mattie's without changing my school clothes or getting a drink.

Sukie met me with a *prrr-rr-oo*. I was disappointed that Mattie wasn't home. I got a drink of water from the outside faucet. I took off my Tyrolean hat, smoothed the feather the way Mattie had shown me, and put the hat on the porch. I laid down next to the hat to wait for Mattie.

Sukie climbed on top of me and pumped my chest before she folded her paws under her and dozed. I fell asleep too, and woke to hear Mattie's voice.

"Hey, come on, sleepyhead, I need help," Mattie said. "I've been working since early morning and I'm tired."

I rolled over and saw Sukie standing on her hind legs, looking into a grocery bag. I helped carry the groceries and put the stuff away, then I sat on the steps next to Mattie.

"Boy, is this good," Mattie said. "I've had so many people around all day. I need to sit, be still, and find myself again."

I knew what she meant, so we sat for a long time without speaking. At last I thought it would be all right to talk.

"You ever had a part-time boy?" I asked.

Mattie sat a long time before she answered. "No, but I guess we could call you a part-time boy," she said at last.

"I want to be your part-time boy all summer

I ran up the hill and turned into Mattie's drive-way calling to her.

"Mattie, I can go! I can go!"

Mattie ran from the back of the yard. On the wide lawn we grabbed hands and pulled around and around in a circle, our feet making little steps in the center.

"Hurray! Hurray! I have a part-time boy!" Mattie cheered.

I was shouting, I don't know what. Just a lot of crazy noises came out of me. Sukie saw our weird whirling and ran in wide circles around us. Her black and white fur seemed to flash around like a pinwheel.

I don't know how long we were whirling around, but as soon as Mattie and I saw Mom, Dad, Paul, and Carl standing in a row watching us, we stopped. Mattie pulled her long hair into place. I picked up my hat, which had fallen to the ground. Dad came over to Mattie with his hand outstretched.

"Good evening, Miss Swenson," he said.

Mattie shook his hand. "It's Mattie," she said. "Jamie and I are both so happy he can come to the country that we had to let the joy come out."

"I understand," Dad said with a big grin.

and live in your part-time house. Please, Mattie. My brothers are going to Jamboree. I want to go with you."

Mattie turned and looked at me. Her blue eyes seemed to see deep into me.

"It sounds good, Jamie," she said. "I'll have to ask your mom and dad if you can come. They'll miss you."

I hadn't thought about asking Mom and Dad. Gee, they didn't even know Mattie. What would they say? Would they let me go?

CHAPTER
4

The next evening, in the middle of our noisy dinner, Dad picked up his spoon and tapped his coffee cup, making it sound like a bell. Everyone stopped eating and looked at him.

"You two keep quiet," he said, pointing the spoon toward Paul and Carl. Dad looked at me. "Jamie, a friend of yours came to see Mom and me today."

I twisted in my chair as I nodded. I could guess what was coming.

"Miss Swenson, from Hill Road, came to see us," Mom butted in. "She'd like you to go with her to her summer home. Would you like that?"

I nodded quickly.

Dad put out his hand and closed it over mine. "Tell us about Miss Swenson," he said.

Before I could start, Paul spoke.

"You mean Miss Swenson who's in charge of the Natural Science Center? She's cool."

"Yeah, she took our class to the Salt Marsh. Boy, she sure knows a lot and she's fun," Carl said.

"How'd you meet her?" Paul asked.

I sat up real straight, took a deep breath and started at the beginning. I told them about climbing the hill in my hat, and about Sukie finding me and taking me to Mattie. No one interrupted. Paul and Carl stopped eating to listen. I went on telling them about the part-time animals, the vegetable garden, being a carpenter's helper and everything. Carl and Paul were looking at me as if I were a stranger.

"Gee, that sounds great, Jamie," Dad said when I had finished. "I vote in favor of your spending the summer with Miss Swenson. By the way, Miss Swenson wants us to visit her this evening."

"Can we go too?" Carl asked.

"That's the plan," replied Dad with a big grin.

I couldn't eat any more. I wanted to get going, to tell Mattie the good news. At last everyone was ready. Dad said we would walk up to Mattie's house and I would lead the way.

Mom said nothing, she just nodded and smiled. Carl and Paul stood there, looking about. They were the watchers now. Mattie asked me to show everyone around the place while she fixed lemonade and cookies.

Carl and Paul were keen on the rabbit hutch. Cinnamon and Ginger had gone home a couple of weeks before, but two white rabbits from the Natural Science Center were now staying in the hutch. Mom liked the part-time goat, which was in the fenced-in yard. The goat bleated and tried to eat Mom's dress when she scratched its bony head. Sukie followed everywhere.

Mattie came outside to say that lemonade and cookies were ready. Sukie ran ahead of us to the house. Before we went inside, Mattie turned on the water so that the walking sprinkler could water the back lawn.

Inside, I looked around. Books, tools, clothes, and dirty dishes were gone. There was a cloth and flowers on the table. The sink was empty. Mattie winked at me when no one was looking. I knew the wink meant that we were on company manners tonight.

When we finished our lemonade and cookies, Paul and Carl looked at some of Mattie's maga-

zines. There were pictures in them of Arizona, where they were going to Jamboree. They let me look too. Sukie tried to lie on top of whatever we were reading until we played with her. Mom, Dad, and Mattie talked and talked.

When it was time to go home, Dad walked over to the door. "That's strange," he said. "It sounds like rain on the porch."

"Oh, my gosh!" exclaimed Mattie. "We're trapped! Trapped by the walking sprinkler. It's walked right up to the house. Don't open the door or we'll have a flood."

"How'll we get out?" Carl asked.

"That's the only door," explained Mattie, taking off her sandals. "I'll climb out the window and turn off the water."

Mattie climbed over the sill of the side window and disappeared into the darkness. Sukie got to the window before Carl, Paul, and I did. We looked out to see Mattie at the corner of the house, turning off the water. She came back in through the door, laughing and shaking water from her hair.

"Water's off," she said. "Never thought I'd get trapped by a mechanical water sprinkler."

Everybody laughed.

After that night, Mattie and I were busy getting ready to go to the country. I helped mulch the garden with hay.

"It's like putting a blanket on the ground," Mattie told me. "You keep the moisture in the earth, and weeds do not grow."

Mattie worked on her station wagon, changing the oil and cleaning the spark plugs so that the wagon would be ready for our ride to the country.

It was crazy wild at our house the day Paul and Carl left for Jamboree. I sat on the porch swing, out of everyone's way, and watched. Several of Carl and Paul's friends were going to Jamboree, so there was a lot of running in and out of the house. When everything was just about ready, Carl came and sat next to me.

"Get a load of that guy," he said, pointing toward Paul, who was marching around acting like he was a general in charge of an army. Carl got up and stretched. He looked down at me. "Have a good summer," he said.

"You, too," I answered.

Carl turned and jumped down all the porch steps at one time.

With Carl and Paul gone, the house was strange and still. The next day I would go away with

Mattie. I didn't eat much dinner because I was excited. Mom, Dad, and I sat on the side porch after dinner. They talked a little, but not much. Mom didn't tell me to go to bed even when the stars came out.

When I did go up to bed, I couldn't sleep. I heard Mom and Dad come upstairs together. They came into my room. They knew I was awake, so they sat on the bed.

"You're going to have to rough it with Miss Swenson," Dad said. "There's no phone, no electricity, no running water, no television—"

"And no bed," I interrupted. "I'm going to sleep in a bag on a soldier's cot."

"Sounds good to me," Dad said.

"I'm afraid you'll be lonesome," Mom said. "There'll be no other children." Her voice sounded different.

"I'll have Sukie, Mattie, and me for company," I told her.

Dad started talking about camping when he was a boy. I lay on my stomach, and Mom rubbed my back. I didn't hear much of what Dad said because I fell asleep.

CHAPTER
5

I woke the next morning before it was light and couldn't go back to sleep. I got up after a while and pulled my clothes on. I put on my Tyrolean hat and walked downstairs to sit and wait on the bottom step in the hall.

Mom and Dad were surprised to find me there. I couldn't eat; I was too excited.

I had gear to take along. Mom and Dad had spent nearly a whole evening talking with Mattie about what I would need. My gear was an old sleeping bag of Paul's. Dad had rolled it up tightly and tied the strings around it. Mom had filled an old duffel bag with my clothes. Dad lifted my gear into the back of our station wagon, and off we went.

Mattie was outside her house, waiting for us. I didn't see Sukie anywhere.

"Where's Sukie?" I asked.

Mattie explained that Sukie had been fed and had her early morning run in the garden. Now she was in her carrying box in the car. Mattie knew that Sukie did not like riding in the car and so she wanted to make sure Sukie didn't hide at the last minute.

Dad put my gear in the back of Mattie's wagon.

"Climb aboard," Mattie ordered.

Mom grabbed me and kissed me. Dad picked me up and squeezed the breath out of me before he put me into the front seat.

"Have fun," he said. "Good-bye, good-bye."

The engine vroomed, and we started down the hill. Mom and Dad stood waving and calling as we went.

Soon we were on strange roads. I got sleepy. My stomach felt empty. I wished I'd eaten breakfast. Going away wasn't as much fun as I'd thought. I didn't say a word. Neither did Mattie. I wondered what was wrong when Mattie pulled the car off the road into a parking area.

"My stomach is growling," she said. "Let's eat."

Mattie reached around the seat and lifted a box up to the front of the car. It was filled with sandwiches, cookies, fruit, and a thermos of milk. We ate without speaking. We hadn't finished when Sukie started meowing, softly at first but then louder and louder.

Mattie released a lever so that my seat would go back. She pushed up the latch on Sukie's box, lifted the lid, and out climbed Sukie. She came right to me.

"You two croodle down on the seat and get some sleep. Sukie will be quiet and still if she's next to you," Mattie said.

I lay down on the seat, and Sukie came close and snuggled up to me. I put my arm over her, and she purred. Soon I was asleep.

I woke when the car started bumping around. I sat up and looked about. Sukie had left me and was standing on her hind legs, looking out the side window. We were on a narrow road with trees all around. The road turned, and at the end of it I could see a house made of logs.

"Here we are," Mattie said as she opened the car door.

Out jumped Sukie. I just sat where I was and looked around. There was a big green field in back and great big rocks high up on one side of the house. Everywhere else there were trees, trees, trees.

We walked down to an old apple orchard to get the kinks out of us after the long car ride. At one side of the orchard Mattie showed me an old foundation of a house. All kinds of plants were growing in it, but I could see the flat stones that had made the cellar wall.

"See, there in the center," Mattie said, pointing. "Those huge stones were the chimney base. Probably they were dragged here by oxen. I believe the house had two rooms with one chimney heating both of them. Rabbits, snakes, and sometimes groundhogs still make their home in the old foundation."

We went back to the new house, where we would live. I helped unload the station wagon. At the front of the house, scrap wood was piled high, left there from some building that had been done in the spring. We had to scramble and slide over the wood to get into the house.

Mattie showed me around and helped me put up the soldier's cot in a room where there was a big stone fireplace. It all seemed strange and exciting to me.

Mattie told me that we'd have a fire in the fireplace every evening and that I was to be in charge of the fire. I knew from the way she said it that this was an important job. I listened carefully as she showed me how to lay a fire and get it started.

When the fire was bright, we sat in front of it and ate the rest of the sandwiches. I was happy but sleepy. Mattie must have noticed, because she asked if I'd like to climb into my sleeping bag. She meant, did I want to go to bed? I nodded, got into my pajamas, and climbed into my bag—only to find Sukie already there, making the bag warm for me. As we snuggled down together, Sukie's double purr filled the room. The good feeling was there.

Mattie wrapped herself in a sleeping bag and sat in a big rocking chair. The flames from the fire made lights move across the dark room. Mattie talked softly. I was going to like it here.

"You've seen a lot of new sights today, Jamie," Mattie said. "Tonight you may hear new sounds."

I listened, but there was only the night stillness to be heard.

"Later," Mattie went on, "owls will call, foxes are sure to bark, and you may hear the sound of someone sawing wood. When this house was new, I heard that sound. I was frightened by it. Who could be sawing wood by moonlight? I tip-toed to the door to find out. I saw a big porcupine

PART-TIME BOY

sitting on its haunches, eating plywood. Porcupines like the glue that holds the layers of wood together. This porcupine had heard me move, and so it stopped eating and gnashed its teeth, making a clicking noise. It was warning me not to come near."

Mattie laughed softly as she remembered. She went on with her story.

"The porcupine didn't need to worry. I wasn't going out! It turned its back toward me and raised its quills as a tiny porcupine came out of the shadows. The large porcupine didn't move for a while, and as I watched, its quills slowly fell back into place. The tiny porcupine came to the big one, and gently they rubbed noses. You see, that is the only way the barbed animals can touch their young ones to show their love. There is plywood outside tonight, and so I wouldn't be surprised if we hear porcupines eating."

"Will you wake me if you hear them?" I asked.

"Of course," replied Mattie.

We never knew if any porcupines came to eat that night because we both slept until Sukie woke us in the morning.

CHAPTER

6

Next day, after breakfast, we cleared the pile of wood that blocked the path to the door. The smaller pieces I piled near the woodshed. Later, Mattie said I was to split them for kindling to start the evening fire. I was puzzled when I found a big piece of wood with a ragged half-circle cut in it.

"Hey, Mattie," I called. "Look at this."

Mattie came over to see. "That is plywood gnawed by a porcupine," she explained.

I looked closely at the wood. It was many thin layers of wood glued together like a sandwich.

"You mean an animal has teeth strong enough to eat the hard wood?" I asked Mattie, who was kneeling on the ground looking for something.

"Ah, here's what I wanted," she announced,

holding up what looked like a needle. "This is a porcupine quill. Here, open your hand so you can hold it while you take a good look."

I held the quill in my hand. It was black with a white tip.

"See the little barb on the end?" asked Mattie.

I looked closely and saw a tiny hook on one end. "It's like a tiny fishhook," I said.

"That's right, Jamie. That barb is what makes the quill dangerous. If the quill gets into an animal's flesh, it works its way deeper and deeper. The hook won't let the animal pull the quill out. So never go near a porcupine—you or Sukie," she said, turning back to her work.

Clearing the wood made us hungry. As soon as we'd made a wide path, Mattie got me to help make sandwiches. We took them out and sat on the doorstep, eating.

"We have to go for supplies this afternoon," Mattie said as we finished.

At home that meant going to the supermarket with Mom, which I didn't like.

"Don't wrinkle your nose at me, Jamie," Mattie said. "You're going to enjoy going for supplies. It will be a surprise for you."

We cleared the lunch things away. I grabbed

my hat, and we were off. Mattie drove slowly up the mountain.

"We're going to a farm—that's the surprise," Mattie explained. "You're going to like these people. Their ancestors settled this farm when Indians still lived in these hills. The parents, grandparents, and great-grandparents of these people, farmers all, worked this same land. I believe those early settlers were like you and me. They liked to live alone and use their imagination to solve their problems."

We rode for a while in silence. I was busy looking at the road, which seemed to get smaller and steeper. Suddenly we were in a flat place with rocky fields as far as I could see.

"Early farmers settled on the hilltops so they could tell if anyone was coming. I get milk, butter, and eggs from today's farmers. You'll like the whole family."

I didn't know about that. I was happy with just Mattie and Sukie.

There were some large trees ahead of us, and through them I could see a white house and a barn. Mattie turned the wagon into a wide road going toward the house and barn. On the porch of the house a couple of dogs stood up to watch the car as we drove toward the big barn. Outside the barn were tractors, trucks, chickens, ducks, cats, and lots of kids.

"Hello, where is everyone?" Mattie called as she stepped out of the wagon.

The kids stopped playing and stared. The dogs came running over from the house, barking. Out of the wide door of the barn stepped a tall, skinny man who was wiping his hands on a cloth.

"Hello, Mattie," he greeted her with a big grin. "Nice to see yah."

I slumped down in the car, watching them while they shook hands and talked. After a while, Mattie turned and crooked her finger at me.

"Come on, Jamie. Meet the Valentines," she said.

I got out slowly. I hate to meet people, especially a lot of people at once. Mattie put her hand on my shoulder and gave it a squeeze.

"Jamie, these are the Valentines," she said, bowing to all of them. "Valentines, meet Jamie, my part-time boy."

I stood there and said nothing, but then, none of them spoke to me either. It didn't seem to matter. Mr. Valentine started walking toward the house with Mattie.

"Mother is inside," he explained. "Come along, everyone. Time for a sit down and somethin' to eat."

The kids moved along. They glanced at me, but they said nothing. I felt sad. I thought Mattie was doing what Mom would do. Mattie was trying to get me to play with other kids. In disgust, I kicked a large stone that was by my side of the path. Mattie's just like everyone else, I thought.

Mrs. Valentine met us at the kitchen door. "You two young 'uns double up so there's a chair for Jamie," she told the two smallest kids.

We all sat around the table drinking cold milk and eating cake. The grown-ups laughed a lot and talked. The kids ate, watched me, and said nothing.

Mattie didn't tell me to go out and play with the boys or ask if I'd like them to come and play with me. Maybe I'd been wrong about Mattie. Maybe all she wanted was a visit with her friends and to get supplies. I felt better and sneaked a closer look at the kids. They all looked alike. They were skinny, with thick curly blond hair and big blue eyes. A couple of times, I caught the tallest boy looking at me, but we didn't speak.

When it was time to go, Mattie had eggs, butter, milk, a loaf of bread, new potatoes, and fresh peas in a big basket.

"Let me cut a piece of chocolate cake for the boy," Mrs. Valentine said. "Never knew a boy who couldn't use a piece of cake."

She cut a big piece of cake and wrapped it carefully. As she handed it to me, she gave me a big smile.

Mattie and I rode down the mountain without a word. When we got home, Sukie rubbed all over my legs; she was glad to have us back.

"We'll have scrambled eggs, new peas, and potatoes for dinner," Mattie said. "It makes me hungry just to think about it."

I got the fire going in the fireplace while Mattie cooked on the campstove in the kitchen. We carried the food to the fireside to eat. When we finished, Mattie stretched and sighed with happiness.

"I thought we'd have a porcupine watch tonight," Mattie said. "We'll zip ourselves into our bags to keep nice and warm while we watch to see if any porcupines come to have a plywood dinner."

The moon was a round yellow ball when it came over the trees, and it lighted the clearing.

We waited a long time. I was just getting sleepy when a small porcupine waddled up to the scrap pile and sniffed around.

"That's a young one. That's why it's so small," whispered Mattie.

"It looks cute enough to pet," I whispered back.

"That's what you think," Mattie replied. "Remember the barbed quill? Never touch a porcupine."

The porcupine must have heard us talking because it waddled on into the shadows without eating.

"Why do porcupines walk so funny?" I asked Mattie as I hopped along in my bag to get to my cot.

"Because they're pigeon-toed," Mattie explained. "They walk like this."

With her toes turned in, Mattie put one foot in front of the other, then took a small step. She looked so funny I started giggling. And as Mattie watched me hopping along in the sleeping bag, she giggled.

"We're two funny animals. You're a porcupine and I'm a kangaroo," I said.

"I can tell we have to get rid of all that scrap

wood if we want to be free of porcupines," Mattie said after she stopped giggling.

All the next morning we loaded scraps of plywood onto the wagon and took it to the town landfill. We were hot and tired when we finished. We set off to the lake for a swim, which was also to be a bath.

The water was cold and clear. We splashed about in it for a long time. We had just climbed on the big rocks at the edge of the lake to dry off when a red truck stopped on the road. The door opened and out jumped Mr. Valentine.

"Hi, Mattie! I thought it was you and the boy," he said, coming toward us.

Mattie walked over to meet him and told him of our morning's work.

"Young Willie is up in the truck. I reckon he'd like to call a swim a bath." Mr. Valentine laughed. "Come on down, Willie."

Around the truck came the tall, skinny boy I'd seen yesterday. He walked toward us. He didn't say anything, but he gave his head a sort of backward jerk. I moved my head the same way.

Mattie and Mr. Valentine were talking about fishing. I climbed over the rocks to the small sandy beach at the edge of the lake, and Willie followed me without saying a word. We started to build a road, making mountains of sand for the road to go over. Then Mr. Valentine called for Willie to go home.

"Let him stay," Mattie said. "Jamie and I'll bring him along when we go home."

"That's fine with me," said Mr. Valentine. "The boy don't get much chance to go lake swimming. He can swim in his underwear."

I heard the big truck drive off while Willie and I were playing in the wet sand. We didn't talk at all, but somehow I knew Willie was having a good time, the same as me. We played for a long time, and the sun was hot on our backs before Mattie came over.

"I hate to stop you guys," Mattie said, "but we have to get home you know."

Willie stripped down to his underwear. We splashed about for a while and then Mattie said we could swim way out in the lake if we stayed alongside her. Out there, the water was cold and black, but it was exciting. When we had had enough, we swam back to the beach, rubbed ourselves down, and changed to dry clothes. Then we took Willie back to the farm.

PART-TIME BOY

CHAPTER
7

We weren't back in the house long when Sukie made a noise she'd never made before. She growled. Mattie heard her too, and so we both ran to the door to see what was upsetting the cat. We saw a large raccoon coming along the road.

"It's searching for its evening meal," Mattie told me.

Sukie jumped up on the table where she arched her back and spit. All her hairs stood on end. She looked scary, like a Halloween cat.

Mattie clapped her hands and knocked her foot against the wooden frame of the screen door. "Go away! Git!" she yelled.

The raccoon didn't care. It came up the steps and stood on its hind legs with its small front paws dangling. For several minutes it looked first at Mattie, then at me, before it turned and ran off across the field.

Mattie sighed. "We're going to have to keep Sukie indoors in the evenings. The raccoon will come back, and Sukie might get into a fight with it. A raccoon could kill her."

I woke that night and missed the warmth of Sukie in my sleeping bag. I propped myself up on my elbow to look around in the moonlight. Where could she have gone? Then, to my surprise, I saw her sitting at the screen door. Outside, something was crying like a baby.

Without making a sound, I slipped out of my bag and crept over to see what was going on. I never expected to see the small porcupine crouched there, its nose to the outer side of the door, crying softly. Sukie stood up and rubbed against my leg. The porcupine turned and waddled into the darkness.

Next morning, I told Mattie about the visiting porcupine. When night came, she listened too, and sure enough the small porcupine came to visit Sukie. Every evening after that, Sukie would go to the screen door and crouch nose to nose with the porcupine.

PART-TIME BOY

Mattie thought Sukie was lonesome for other cats, so she had made a friend of the young porcupine. Mattie and I weren't lonesome. We had ourselves, each other and Sukie. Of course, we saw the Valentines too, when we went for supplies a few times a week.

One hot morning when we went to the farm I walked over to the barn in search of Willie. He was inside, moving bales of hay. He usually didn't talk much, so I was surprised when he stopped work and spoke to me.

"I like your hat," he said. "Never saw the likes of that."

"It's a Tyrolean hat. People in Austria wear them," I replied.

"I got a box of arrowheads back at the house. Wanna see them?" he asked.

I nodded.

We went back to the house, through the kitchen, and into the big dining room. Willie stopped at a row of shelves and picked up a flat box filled with cotton wool. In it were six arrowheads made of stone.

"Pick 'em up if you want to," Willie said.

I picked up one after the other. The edges of each arrowhead were kind of rippled.

"I've never seen anything like these," I told Willie. "Where'd you get 'em?"

"On the big rock ledge at Mattie's. You been there?" he asked.

I nodded. Mattie and I walked to the ledge many evenings, but I didn't know that Indians had lived there.

I heard Mattie calling from outside. It was time to go home. I gave Willie the box to put away. We were on the porch, and I was picking up the supply basket when I spoke to Willie.

"Thanks, Willie," I said. "Thanks a lot."

Willie stood rubbing the back of his curly hair with his hand. "So long," he answered me.

That evening, Mattie and I walked the logging trail to the rock ledge. I tried to see the top of the rock ledge as we stood there. I bent back so far that my hat fell off. That ledge was sure big and high.

"Know how those giant rocks got here?" Mattie asked.

I shook my head.

"Long ago, the rock was pushed along to this place by a big sheet of frozen snow called a glacier," Mattie explained. "Indians lived here before the white settlers. When they were hunting deer, they lived in the highest rock ledges because, from there, they could see the deer as they moved about the country. The Indians used the overhanging rock for shelter. I've climbed the rockface and found black marks from the smoke of Indian fires on the top ledge."

"Do you think I could climb up and look for arrowheads?" I asked Mattie.

"You couldn't climb the rockface by yourself," Mattie said. "You'd need someone to show you the best way up. I'll try to go with you later on but, as you know, I took the summer off from my job to get my house finished. The next thing I want to do is get a sink in the kitchen. It's such a nuisance to have to carry all the waste water outside."

I knew we needed a sink because I sloshed water on the floor whenever I tried to carry the basin out-of-doors.

"We'll get a sink from a junkyard," Mattie said, "and we'll work hard to put it in. *Then* we'll climb the rock. O.K.?"

I nodded. Going to a junkyard sounded like fun.

Next day we went to three junkyards before Mattie found the sink she wanted. The sink was so big and heavy, it took three men to slide it in the back of the wagon. We couldn't move it, and so we had to ride everywhere with the sink in the car. When we went to the Valentines, Mr. and Mrs. Valentine came out to take a look at the sink. Willie wanted to take a look too.

After a few minutes, he turned to me. "Want to see a new calf?" he asked.

I nodded.

We raced over to the barn, and I got there first. I waited till Willie came and led me down a narrow flight of wooden steps. We walked along a ways, and there in a stall, on fresh straw, a young calf lay. It was beautiful.

"May I touch it?" I asked.

Willie nodded.

I stooped and stroked the calf's side. It wasn't soft like Sukie.

In the next stall a large cow made a terrible noise and started moving about as much as it could.

"That's the mother and she doesn't want us here," Willie said.

We backed away and went up through the barn to find Mattie just about ready to leave.

All the way home I kept thinking about Willie. I liked him. He liked me. I'd made a friend without talking a lot.

PART-TIME BOY

CHAPTER

8

Now that we had the sink, Mattie had to build the frame on which the sink would rest. One hot day I said I'd make sandwiches for lunch so that she could go on working.

"Gee, thanks, Jamie," Mattie said. "The frame will be ready today. We'll need a few people to help lift the sink into place."

I sliced the homemade bread we got from Mrs. Valentine and spread it with butter. I was cutting cheese and tomatoes to put on the bread when the noontime quiet was broken. A car came *thump, thump, bump* up our hill. The horn was tooting and a man was shouting.

"*Yahoo!* Anybody home?" he called.

Around the curve bounced a green jeep with long orange bicycle markers waving on either side of the windscreen. Mattie dropped her hammer and ran out the door even before the jeep screeched to a stop. I watched as a big man leaped out of the jeep. When Mattie got to him, he put his hands under her arms and lifted her high in the air. After he put her down, they walked over and looked at the jeep.

Now that we had company for lunch, I made two more sandwiches. I looked again at the man, who was sitting on the back of the wagon with Mattie, and decided to leave the cheese, tomatoes, bread, and milk on the table. He'd eat a lot.

I saw Sukie come out from under a hemlock where she had been hiding from the heat. Sukie was rubbing against the man's boots.

I went to the door, and taking a deep breath called, "Lunch is ready. Come and eat it before it gets hot." I sounded like my mom.

Mattie and the man looked up.

"Oh, Jamie," Mattie said, jumping down. "I'm truly sorry. I forgot you were here."

"Who's that?" the man asked.

"I'm Jamie, Mattie's part-time boy," I answered before Mattie could speak.

"Hi, Jamie. I'm Mike," the man said, walking toward the house.

PART-TIME BOY

Sukie ran ahead of him through the open door, giving me a *prrr-rr-oo* as she passed.

We sat down and started eating. Mike ate his two sandwiches before I had finished half of mine. He went right on eating till all the cheese, most of the bread, and all the leftover pie were gone. He picked up the pitcher and drank the milk right down. I was right. He ate a lot.

Mattie and Mike talked and talked. I watched Mattie's blue eyes sparkle. She was happy. I never heard her talk so much. I listened while Sukie sat on my knees, purring loudly. Sukie likes people to talk.

"You always have so much to say?" Mike asked, turning to me.

I shrugged.

"Jamie is not overly talkative," Mattie told him. "Jamie only says what he has to."

"That's a good idea," Mike said as he got up from the table. He walked over to the sink frame and stood looking at it with his hands on his hips.

"Frame finished?" he asked Mattie. "If so, I'll move the sink in place."

"Sink's heavy," Mattie said.

Mike went out to the wagon, pulled the long sink toward him, and lifted it. He carried it through the door I held open. Gee! He was strong.

Slowly, carefully, he set the sink in the frame. Mattie was proud of her work. She clapped her hands and jumped up and down.

"This calls for a celebration," Mike said. "We'll have a feast. Jamie and I'll go get food and cook while you get the pipe in to carry water away from the house." He turned to me as he headed for the jeep. "Climb aboard, Jamie. Let's go!"

Golly, without asking to, I was going to ride in the jeep. I grabbed my hat and ran out to climb in the jeep. Mike followed and hopped into the driver's seat.

"Hold tight!" he shouted as the engine vroomed.

Mike turned the jeep, and we bumped down the rutted road. The town road was smooth so we went faster and faster. The wind was blowing, and I had to hold my hat as tightly as I held the seat. Wow! This was more exciting than driving a make-believe stagecoach.

Mike bought lots of food. After we put the grocery bags in the jeep, we walked along the main street because Mike wanted to find a hardware store.

"I want to get an Arctic Boy," he explained.

I didn't know what he was talking about. Mattie had me, she didn't need another boy.

"Mike," I said as I ran along next to him, "I'm the only boy Mattie wants."

Mike laughed so loud that people stopped and looked. "An Arctic Boy is like a barrel," he explained. "It holds water and keeps it cool. It has a little faucet to let the water out. It'll help Mattie to have a water supply at the sink."

We found an Arctic Boy in the hardware store, and as Mike carried it back to the jeep I got to thinking I'd like to fool Mattie the way Mike had kind of fooled me. When the jeep was climbing the hill, I asked Mike, "Can I tell Mattie about the Arctic Boy?"

"Yeah, sure," Mike answered, nodding.

The jeep had hardly stopped when I jumped down and ran inside to Mattie.

"We got a boy for you," I called.

"A boy? What kind of boy?" Mattie asked.

"An Arctic Boy," I answered.

Mattie was puzzled. "An Eskimo boy?" she asked.

Mike came through the door carrying the large

aluminum barrel. "Here's your Arctic Boy." He laughed.

"You fooled me, Jamie," Mattie said.

Mike put the Arctic Boy next to the sink and filled it with water from one of our jerry cans. He put a basin in the sink because the pipe wasn't finished yet.

"You run the first water, Jamie," he said.

I reached up and turned the faucet. The water ran into the basin. Sukie, hearing the running water, leaped to the edge of the sink and took a drink as the water came out.

"That cat thinks we did it just for her," Mike said.

Mattie went on with her plumbing chores. Mike let me help put up his tent and I helped him make a ring of stones for a fire, too.

It was nearly dark when everything was ready. Mattie shut Sukie in the house before we started to eat in the firelight.

As we were eating corn, the raccoon came out of the shadows. It stood on its hind legs, watching us closely.

"Brazen, isn't it?" Mike asked as he threw a half-eaten ear of corn toward the raccoon. The animal grabbed it and ran off.

PART-TIME BOY

"Good thing Sukie's shut in the house," Mattie said, wiping some melted butter off her chin.

When we couldn't eat any more, we sat close together for warmth. I saw the small porcupine waddle up to the door to sit nose to nose with Sukie. I nudged Mike and pointed toward the house. Mike saw the porcupine in the moonlight at the door.

"Don't let a porcupine worry you," Mike told me. "Porcupines are friendly animals. A friend of mine used to look out her kitchen window when she was washing dishes to watch the birds at the feeder. One day she noticed a strange shape in the back of the yard. Going out for a closer look, she found a small porcupine. She watched all day but never saw a mother porcupine about. In the evening she took a small doll's nursing bottle, filled it with milk, and offered it to the porcupine. The baby got the idea and sucked at the bottle. When the milk was gone, it cried for more. It wasn't long before the little porcupine could hold the bottle in its long claws and feed itself.

"The porcupine became a pet and stayed about the yard. One day my friend, who had been cutting brush and had on a heavy jacket and gloves, came through the yard and the porcupine

waddled up to her. Being well protected against its quills, my friend picked the porcupine up and smoothed its stomach. The porcupine liked that.

"That porcupine stayed for years. Became a real pet and would come to the door crying for potato chips. Porcupines like salt, you see."

"Let's get this straight," Mattie interrupted. "No potato chips for this porcupine. Here, all animals stay wild."

"*My* friend would hold a potato chip between her lips and let the porcupine take it," Mike said, poking me with his elbow to show that he was teasing Mattie.

We watched the young porcupine back away from the door. The fire became a red glow. The stars were so bright that I thought I could reach up and pick them out of the sky. Treefrogs sang along with the insects. Owls called to us as we walked to the house together.

Sukie had my sleeping bag warm when I crawled in beside her. Sukie purred loudly. She was happy, and so was I. I had another friend— Mike.

CHAPTER
9

It was different with Mike around.

"Sandwiches for breakfast, sandwiches for lunch. How can you stand it?" Mike asked Mattie one morning when he came from his tent.

"I'm too busy to cook," Mattie said. "Besides, Jamie makes good sandwiches, so that's what we eat."

"Jamie'd make a good cook," Mike replied. "Come on, Jamie, I'll teach you."

Soon I could fry bacon crisp, turn eggs over lightly, and fry potatoes.

"You're a quick learner, Jamie," Mike said after lunch one day.

I grinned at him. I liked messing around the campstove.

Two mornings a week, Mike drove off in his jeep to go to school. When I asked Mike why he went to school he told me he went to talk about digging.

Mattie interrupted. "Mike goes to school because he got left back," she said teasing. Mike rolled up his paper napkin and threw it at her. They never did answer me.

Evenings before dinner we played soccer on the road. Wow! Mike was good. Mattie played well too, but Mike could make the ball go anywhere he wanted it to. One night I watched as Mike ran under the ball. He leaped high in the air and twisted his head as it touched the ball. The ball went spinning to Mattie. I ran over to Mike.

"Show me, show me how, Mike. I want to do that too," I pleaded.

"O.K. Jamie, I'll show you how to do that," Mike promised.

Every evening after that Mike taught me. He showed me the right way to put my foot under the ball so I could kick it wherever I wished. He helped me practice spinning the ball with a turn of my head. Most fun of all was when he taught me to capture the ball with my knee, let it roll down my leg, and then trap it with my feet. That was a real neat trick.

When we finished dinner we'd sit by the fire

while Mike told stories. He knew about so many different things I wondered why he was still going to school, but I didn't ask again.

One day I was practicing soccer by myself when Mike came back from school. Willie was beside him in the jeep. I didn't know they knew each other.

"Hey, Willie," I called.

Willie jumped down and gave that backward jerk of his head, which meant hello.

"After lunch Willie is going to do some excavating of the Indian ledge," Mike explained. "He's got his equipment in his knapsack."

"Can I go with him, please?" I begged.

"Oh, yes, Jamie," Mattie said. "You've waited a long time to climb the ledge."

Willie and I ate fast, not saying a word. We wanted to get started.

"You'd better have some equipment if you want to help," Mike said to me after we cleared the table. He put a trowel, a sieve, and a paintbrush in a small knapsack for me.

Our packs on our backs, Willie and I walked off down the logging trail. We were at the bottom of the rock ledge before long.

"We have to watch our footing so that we don't step on a loose rock and slide back down," Willie told me as he tightened his pack. "You'd better tuck your hat under one of your straps and carry it. If it fell off your head and you grabbed for it, you could fall."

I put my hat safely in my pack.

"Don't pull yourself up on any small trees growing out of the rocks," Willie said, "because they may come loose. Let your legs lift you. Ready? Let's go."

Willie started up the rockface, and I followed. Up and up we went before moving along a narrow ledge. After that we climbed higher and higher. It was scary. We were both out of breath when we pulled ourselves to the top rock with our arms. We sat silently and looked at the treetops below us.

"Come on," Willie said after a few minutes. "I'll show you the cave."

I followed Willie along the wide, flat rock to a narrow path that sloped down. Suddenly we were standing on another wide, flat rock. The big rock we had been on first was hanging out over our heads.

"This is the cave," Willie said. "Come inside and I'll show you where the rock is still black from Indian fires."

I followed Willie into the cave. Looking up, I could see where the roof of the rock cave was black.

As Willie was taking off his pack, I looked around. There were wooden sticks in the floor of the cave with string tied around them, making squares.

"What's that?" I asked, pointing.

"That's where I've made diggings before—where I found the arrowheads. Now, I am going to dig farther back in the cave."

Out of his pack he took more pointed sticks and a ruler. He measured a square and hammered the pointed ends of the sticks into the thin layer of soil on the cave floor. He tied the string tightly around the sticks.

"Mike showed me how to do this," he explained as he worked. "Mike is an archaeologist." He said the word carefully. "That means he studies things that men made in the past."

"Is that why he goes to school?" I asked.

"He goes to school to teach people how to

make diggings and record what they find," Willie replied.

Archaeologist, I said to myself. I liked the sound of that.

"Could I be an archaeologist?" I asked.

"I guess so," Willie said. "It's not like making roads and mountains in the sand. It's digging to find out about real people of long ago."

Willie worked as he talked. He'd take a trowel full of earth, put it in his sieve, and shake away the loose earth, leaving small stones and acorns in the sieve. "You do this over and over until you find something," he said.

I tried it for a while with my trowel and sieve, but it wasn't much fun. I got up and walked along to the end of the cave.

Willie gave a shout.

"Oh boy! Look, Jamie, look!" he cried.

I ran back. He had a small round gray thing in his sieve.

"What is it?" I asked.

"I think it's the bowl of a clay Indian pipe," he said. "I've seen them in museums."

He reached in his knapsack and took out a clear plastic box and put the pipe bowl in it carefully.

Willie's hands were shaking with excitement. He silently measured inside the square and wrote in his notebook where he had found the pipe bowl. Then he sat back, grinning and rubbing the back of his curly head. We were both excited.

"Let's go right back and show Mike," Willie said.

Quickly we put our tools away and climbed down the rockface. We ran along the logging trail.

At the orchard, I waited for Willie to catch up. I saw Sukie sitting on the lower branch of a tree. I called to her but she didn't move, so I walked over and found it wasn't Sukie at all. It was the small porcupine. With its back to me, the white tips of its black quills looked like the fine lines of white hair on Sukie's back.

Willie went right up to the house. When I got there, he was showing Mike and Mattie his find.

"Good grief!" exclaimed Mike. "It *is* a clay pipe bowl. Good work, Willie."

"Would you take me home to show Pa?" Willie asked.

"Sure, come on," said Mike.

After they had gone, I told Mattie about the young porcupine in the tree. Mattie shook her

head. She didn't believe the porcupine's back looked like Sukie's.

"Don't you see? That's why the porcupine comes here," I insisted. "The porcupine believes Sukie is a porcupine and wants her for a friend."

PART-TIME BOY

CHAPTER
10

It was cold and sunny the morning Mike folded his tent, climbed into his jeep and drove away with the bicycle markers flying in the wind. Mike wasn't coming back. He was going with other archaeologists on a dig in New Mexico which would last all winter. Mattie and I stood silent and sad until the jeep was out of sight, then we walked back to the house together.

Mattie was quiet all morning. I felt sad for her. I decided to cook her a good lunch to make her feel better.

When I went to dump the potato peelings on the compost pile, I saw the young porcupine croodled on the log beside the road where Sukie liked to sun herself. I called Mattie to come see, because the porcupine never came at this time of day. Mattie was upset when she saw the animal.

"Go in the house and keep Sukie there," she

commanded as she marched along the road toward the porcupine.

"Just what do you think you're doing here?" she asked the porcupine as she stooped down. "Cats and porcupines don't mix."

The porcupine lifted its face to Mattie as she stood up.

"Go away!" Mattie ordered. Then she stomped back to the house.

"I think the porcupine is lonesome and wants to rub noses with Sukie 'cause it thinks Sukie is a porcupine," I said.

Mattie didn't answer. When we sat down to lunch, we could see the porcupine through the window. It didn't move.

After lunch, I went outside to sit on the steps.

"Don't go near the porcupine," Mattie warned.

I lowered myself to the step, not answering her. I sat a long time, but the porcupine didn't move. Then Mattie came out with a broom in her hand. I watched her angry figure as she went over to the porcupine and prodded it with the broom.

The porcupine waddled across the meadow, crying as it went. Mattie walked behind the animal, poking it with the broom to keep it moving. I followed.

Just before the porcupine reached the steep bank at the edge of the town road, it rolled itself into a ball. As I watched, I saw the porcupine bump into a tree before rolling down the bank. I went along to the tree and saw some porcupine quills stuck in the bark. They looked like Sukie's fine lines of white hairs.

"Hey, Mattie," I called. "Look at this."

Mattie came and stooped down for a close look. "Well, I'll be," she exclaimed. "It does look like the lines of white on Sukie's back! You were right all the time."

Mattie stood up. "Sukie's *not* a porcupine, she's a *cat!*"

Mattie called after the porcupine as it disappeared in the woods across the road. Mattie laughed as we climbed across the meadow. We both felt happier.

As we went in the door, Sukie ran to greet us with a *prrr-rr-oo*. Mattie picked the cat up and held her in her arms. Mattie rubbed Sukie's head and rocked her back and forth. Sukie purred.

"Sukie, my love, you are *not* a porcupine. Remember that," Mattie said.

Sukie had no answer.

One evening, as I was carrying in more wood

for the fire, Sukie squeezed past my legs and ran into the black night. I called Mattie, but Sukie was gone. I felt awful.

"We'll call her," Mattie said as we went outside.

Sukie didn't come. I even tried tapping her dish with a spoon, a sound that always made her come. But not tonight. We couldn't find her anywhere.

"*Brrr*, it's too cold to stay out here," Mattie said. "Besides, being a cat, she'll come when she is ready and not before."

I was scared. I loved Sukie. She played with me, she shared my bed and food. I didn't want her to get hurt or killed by the raccoon.

"I'm scared, Mattie," I said, feeling tears in back of my eyes and hearing them in my voice.

"Now, Jamie, don't be scared. Sukie can outrun the raccoon. She may decide to run and not to fight. What do you think would happen if she met her porcupine friend and rubbed noses?" Mattie asked, laughing. She was trying to make me feel better.

Wrapped in our sleeping bags, we sat at the screen door watching the moon rise. It was a long time before we heard Sukie's angry growl.

We both saw the raccoon near the steps at the same time. We silently poked each other, and Mattie pointed to the rocks. In the moonlight I could just see Sukie's figure crouched high on the rock. The moon got brighter and made the cat's white fur glisten. My heart banged in my chest with fear when I saw Sukie lash her tail. Standing, the cat arched her back. She spat and hissed, challenging the raccoon to fight. Not far apart, the two masked animals stared at each other.

Click, click, click. The sound made me jump. It was an angry porcupine clicking its teeth. The raccoon and Sukie didn't move.

Out of the shadows the small porcupine wobbled, gnashing its teeth all the time. It came between the two angry animals, turned its back to the raccoon, and raised its quills. I stared. The porcupine looked bigger and bigger. It was scary.

Sukie leaped onto the rock above her and stopped for a second before streaking across the clearing to the side door. I stumbled out of my bag to run and open the door for her. Sukie rushed past me and sat on the mat in front of the fire. Slowly, carefully, she started to wash herself as if nothing had happened.

Mattie and I went to the door to see what was going on. The raccoon was gone, but the porcupine was waddling toward the woods.

"Thank you," I called after the porcupine.

"There's a swagger in its waddle tonight," said Mattie, laughing with relief. "Jamie, I didn't understand. That porcupine is such a faithful friend to Sukie that, whether or not it thinks Sukie is a porcupine, it would protect her."

Before going to sleep, I lay in my bag with Sukie warm and purring beside me and thought how I'd waited all summer to see a porcupine raise its quills. I knew it was something I'd never forget.

After that night, we made sure Sukie didn't get outside after dark.

CHAPTER

11

The day before we were to go home, we rode up to Valentine's farm to say good-bye. Willie and I walked across the meadow and leaned on the split-rail fence, watching the cows.

"I go home tomorrow," I said.

"Yeah," Willie replied, rubbing the back of his head.

"I want you to have my Tyrolean hat," I said, handing it to him. The hat was faded and out of shape, but I knew he still liked it.

Willie grinned and put the hat on his blond curls. He sure looked freaky.

"This is for you," Willie said, reaching in his back pocket and taking out a clear plastic box. In it was one of the arrowheads.

"Thanks, Willie," was all I could say.

Mattie called for me to come, and so Willie and

I raced to the car. As usual, I won. Mr. and Mrs. Valentine and the kids stood in a line to wave and shout good-bye. Willie waved the Tyrolean hat as we turned onto the road.

Next morning I packed my duffel bag, rolled my sleeping bag, and folded the cot. Together, Mattie and I swept out the house and tidied up. Mattie locked the doors and off we went. I took a last look at the house; it looked lonesome and sad.

"Good-bye house, good-bye porcupine," I called out the open car window. I was sure the porcupine was watching us even if we couldn't see it.

I slid down in the seat. I felt funny, sad, and out of place. Summer was gone and here I was, the little guy—going home, saying nothing. Mattie looked sideways at me.

"We'll always have our summer to remember," she said, like she was reading my mind. "Close the window and let Sukie out so that she can sit on your lap. She'd like that."

I loosened my seat belt and reached around to lift the latch of Sukie's box. With a *prrr-rr-oo* she leaped over the seat and onto my knees. Sukie made her double purr, which shows she is really happy. I felt better. I held her till we were nearly home. When we got to our town, I put the cat back in her box.

Our road didn't look any different, the house was the same. Carl and Paul were kicking a soccer ball around the back yard with some other guys.

"Hey, Jamie!" Carl called.

"Here comes the little guy," Paul shouted as the car stopped. They went right on with the game.

Mom burst out the door and ran down the steps. She grabbed me as I got out of the wagon and hugged me tight. She held me with her arms straight out and looked at me.

"How brown you are, and tall. Oh, look at your hair!" The words tumbled out, and she hugged me again. "Jamie, I missed you so much."

It was exciting.

Mattie got out of the car and stretched as I went to the back of the wagon to unload my gear. Carl kicked the ball toward me. I knew that was his way of telling me he was glad I was home. The ball didn't reach the back of the car. Instead, Mattie jumped and flicked the ball with her foot, sending it to the back of the yard.

"Nice shot!" the guys shouted, going after it.

Mattie went on talking to Mom while I carried my gear to the porch. "I won't stay because Sukie is in her box," Mattie explained to Mom. "She doesn't like being in there and will start meowing."

Mattie got back in the car. I walked down the steps, holding out the car keys. I looked at Mattie. Her hair was nearly white from the sun, her face was brown, and her eyes looked so blue.

"Come back soon," I said as she started the engine.

Mattie looked up with a grin, nodded, and backed the car out of the drive.

I opened my sleeping bag and threw it over the porch clothesline to air. I carried the duffel bag into the house and upstairs. My room seemed small and strange. I could hear the guys shouting in the yard.

"I'll have to take you for a haircut tomorrow," Mom said as she came in my room.

"I can walk down myself," I answered.

"Of course you can. I forget you are growing up. I'm going to call Dad now and tell him you're home," she said, turning to go. "He missed you too."

I dumped some of the stuff from my duffel bag on my bed and went to look out the window. The guys were playing soccer. I wondered what would happen if I went out? Would they tease me? I'd have to find out.

I ran downstairs and out the back door. I jumped down all the porch steps at once. I trotted in place, my elbows bent, warming up like Mike had taught me.

"Get it, little guy!" Paul yelled as he kicked the ball high in the air toward me. I ran under the ball, jumped and turned my head, touching the ball and spinning it back to Paul. He didn't expect that. The ball went flying past him. Everyone hollered.

I stood with my hands on my hips watching them go after the ball. Maybe they'd never understand me, but now I knew they'd let me play without teasing.

Paul stood at the back of the yard holding the ball. "It's goin' to be a throw-in," he yelled.

He stood a minute and held the ball over his head. He opened his mouth to shout again but stopped for a second. He looked at me across the yard.

"Jamie, you're on my team. Play center forward," he ordered. I ran into place. Paul tossed the ball into play. The game was on again. Soon, we were all running and playing together.

PART-TIME BOY